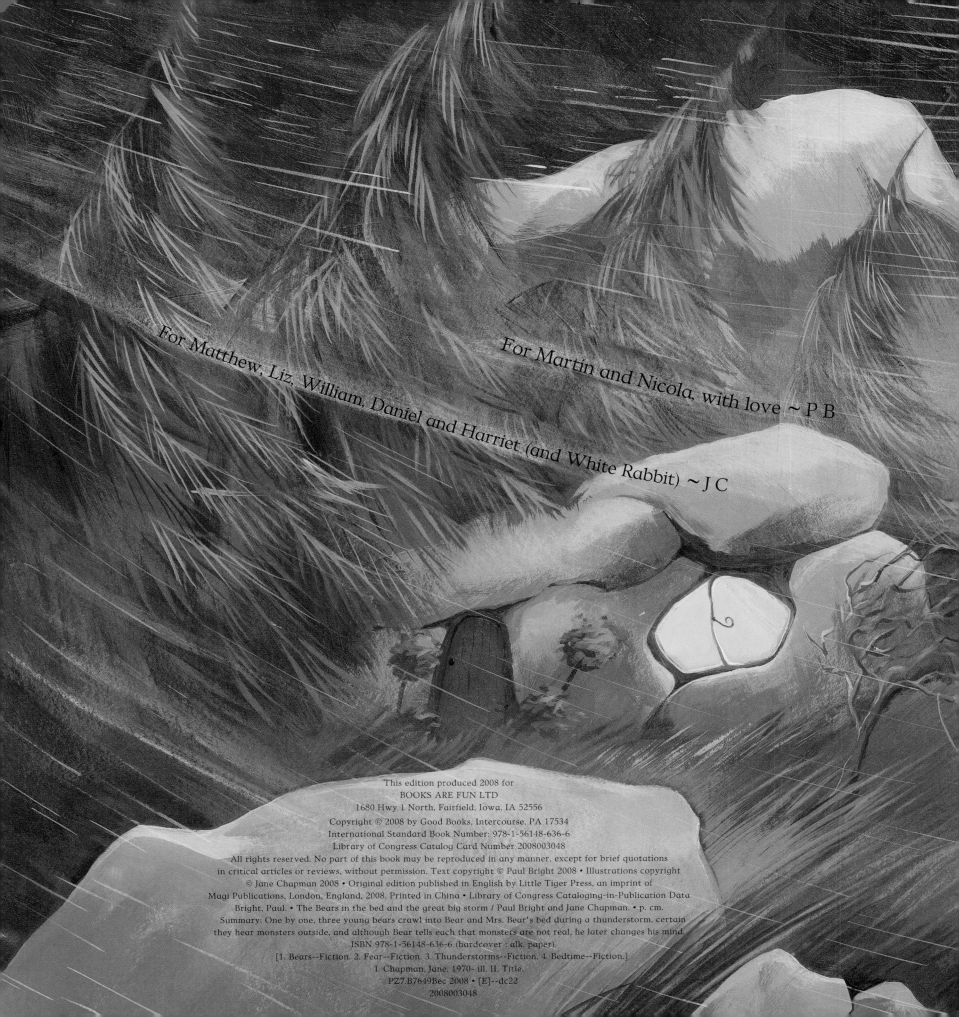

For Matthew, Liz, William, Daniel and Harriet (and White Rabbit) ~ J C

For Martin and Nicola, with love ~ P B

This edition produced 2008 for
BOOKS ARE FUN LTD
1680 Hwy 1 North, Fairfield, Iowa, IA 52556

Copyright © 2008 by Good Books, Intercourse, PA 17534
International Standard Book Number: 978-1-56148-636-6
Library of Congress Catalog Card Number 2008003048

Bright, Paul. • The Bears in the bed and the great big storm / Paul Bright and Jane Chapman. • p. cm.
Summary: One by one, three young bears crawl into Bear and Mrs. Bear's bed during a thunderstorm, certain
they hear monsters outside, and although Bear tells each that monsters are not real, he later changes his mind.
ISBN 978-1-56148-636-6 (hardcover : alk. paper)
[1. Bears--Fiction. 2. Fear--Fiction. 3. Thunderstorms--Fiction. 4. Bedtime--Fiction.]
I. Chapman, Jane, 1970- ill. II. Title.
PZ7.B7649Bec 2008 • [E]--dc22
2008003048

The Bears in the Bed and the Great Big Storm

Paul Bright   Jane Chapman

How the wind blew!

It howled in the treetops, so that the branches bent and creaked and the leaves shivered and shook. It blew over the hills and the high places, howling and wailing through the rocky passes.

Bear and Mrs. Bear slept warm and snug and untroubled in their bed.

Then Bear felt a tugging at his blanket. He opened one eye. There was Baby Bear.

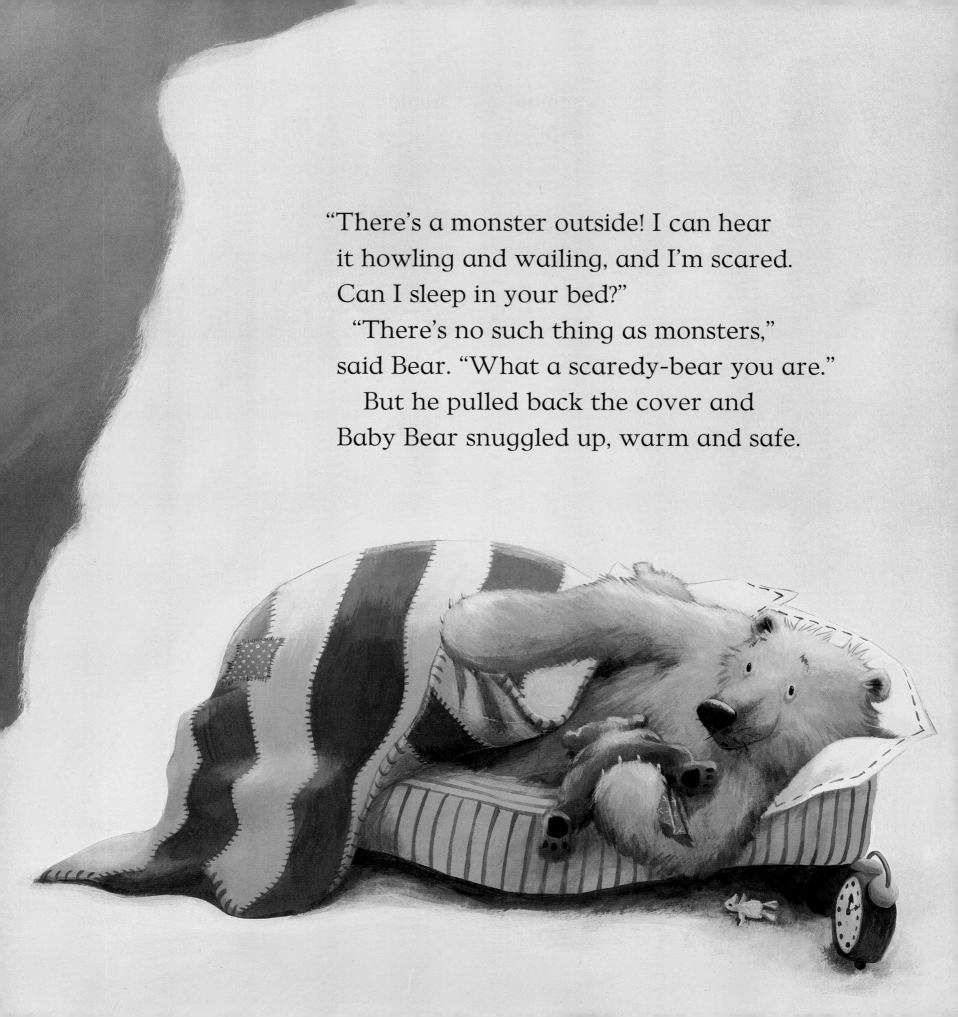

"There's a monster outside! I can hear
it howling and wailing, and I'm scared.
Can I sleep in your bed?"
 "There's no such thing as monsters,"
said Bear. "What a scaredy-bear you are."
But he pulled back the cover and
Baby Bear snuggled up, warm and safe.

How the thunder crashed!

It boomed and crackled so the house
shuddered and the windows rattled.
It grumbled and rumbled and echoed
and faded, only to boom and crash again.

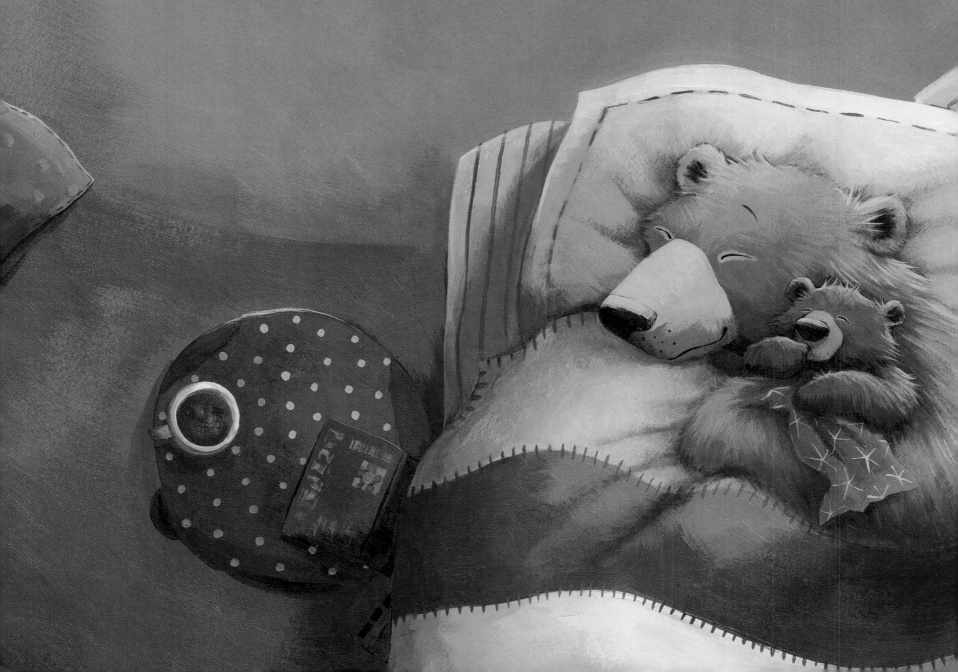

Mrs. Bear and Baby Bear slept warm
and snug and untroubled in their bed.
But Bear lay awake, with his
paws over his ears.

Then Bear felt a tapping on his shoulder. There was Little Bear. "There's a monster outside! Its tummy is rumbling and grumbling like it's going to eat me! Can I sleep with you?"

"There's no such thing as monsters," said Bear. "You're another scaredy-bear." But he lifted the cover and Little Bear snuggled up, warm and safe.

How the lightning flashed!

It forked and flickered, lighting the scurrying clouds and splashing quick, black shadows on the windows and the walls.

Mrs. Bear and Baby Bear and Little Bear slept warm and snug and untroubled in their bed. But Bear lay awake, with his pillow wrapped around his head.

Then Bear felt a tap on his nose. It was Young Bear.

"There's a monster outside! It has huge, twisted horns and it's making shadows on my wall. Can I come and sleep in your bed?"

"There's no such thing as monsters!" cried Bear.
But he let Young Bear climb into the bed, where he snuggled up, warm and safe.

Now Bear was wide awake.

He listened to the wind howling and the thunder crashing. He watched the lightning fork and flash.

"Young Bear's right," he thought. "The shadows on the wall *do* look like monster horns." And he pulled up the bed covers right over his head.

Suddenly, there was a
RAT-TAT-TAT at the door . . .

Everybody woke at once.
"Wh-wh-who can that be?" said Bear.
"It's probably nothing at all," said Mrs. Bear.
"Go and see." And she gave Bear a little push.

Bear climbed nervously out of bed.
He picked up a candle to light his way,
and padded slowly, ever so slowly,
to the door.
  "You're all such scaredy-bears!"
he said to the others. "There's no such
thing as m-m-m-monsters!"

As he turned the handle, the wind blew the door open. The candle went out. And everything was black as black.

Then the lightning flashed . . . .

"A MONSTER!" shouted Bear.
He jumped back in fright and dived
straight under the bed.

"It's not a monster. It's a moose!" said Moose, stepping through the doorway. "The storm has blown my house away. Can I sleep in yours?"

Bear peered out from under the bed.

Baby Bear and Little Bear and Young Bear
laughed and laughed and laughed.

"What a scaredy-bear you are!" they said.

"Don't you know . . .

THERE'S NO SUCH THING AS MONSTERS?!"